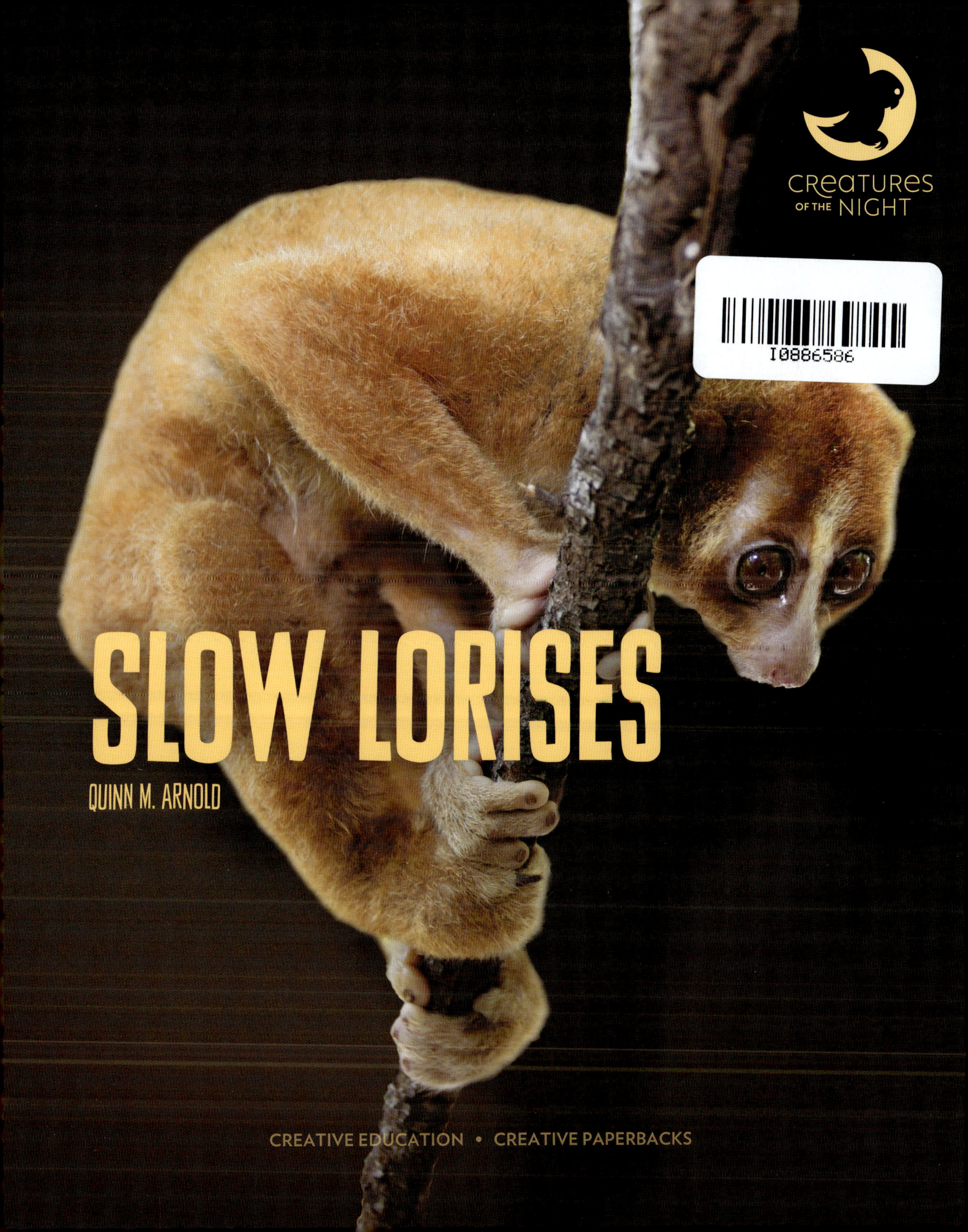

Creatures of the Night

SLOW LORISES

QUINN M. ARNOLD

CREATIVE EDUCATION • CREATIVE PAPERBACKS

CONTENTS

NIGHTFALL CLOAKS A TROPICAL FOREST IN SOUTHEAST ASIA.
A SLOW LORIS STIRS FROM ITS SPOT IN THE FORK OF A TREE.

IT IS HUNGRY. REACHING HAND OVER HAND, THE CREATURE BEGINS ITS STEADY CLIMB.

Slow lorises are tree-dwelling **primates**. Their large, round eyes face forward. In dim light, the eyes glow orange or red. This is called eyeshine. It helps **nocturnal** slow lorises see in the dark.

VENOM
PATCH
VENOM
PATCH

A patch inside each elbow produces **venom**. Slow lorises lick these spots to make their saliva toxic. Their poisonous bite drives away predators.

Slow lorises weigh less than five pounds (2.3 kg). Thick, woolly fur hides their small ears and short tails. A dark stripe runs down their backs. Pale fur marks their flat faces.

Slow lorises eat mostly tree gum and **arthropods**. They scrape away tree bark with their teeth. Then they lick up the oozing gum. Some slow lorises also eat nectar, birds' eggs, fruit, or small animals.

SLOW LORIS DIET

SLOW LORIS TOES

When a slow loris finds prey, it rises up on its hind legs. It grips the branch with its powerful feet. Then it lunges, grabbing its snack with both hands. Slow lorises may hang upside-down as they gobble their food.

A baby slow loris watches its mother and older siblings **forage**. This is how it learns what foods to eat. Slow lorises stay with their mothers for 18 to 24 months.

LIFE OF A SLOW LORIS

BIRTH
pale fur; weighs 1.7 oz (48.2 g)

2–8 WEEKS
able to move around

11 WEEKS
fur darkens to adult colors

6 MONTHS
stops drinking milk

18–24 MONTHS
weighs 3 lbs (1.4 kg); reproduces

20–25 YEARS
end of life

Slow lorises live in home ranges. These areas sometimes overlap. But slow lorises rarely fight. Those that live near each other may play together.

As the sun rises, the slow loris returns to its sleeping spot. Hidden among the leaves, it will be safe from snakes and hawks. The slow loris tucks its head under its arm. Gripping a branch with one foot, it curls into a tight ball. Time to sleep.

LIMBS

short, sturdy, and strong, arms and legs are almost equal lengths

FUR

drab fur blends in with surroundings; a dark stripe runs down the back and a pale streak between the eyes

DIGITS

nails on all but the second toes, which have a claw for grooming

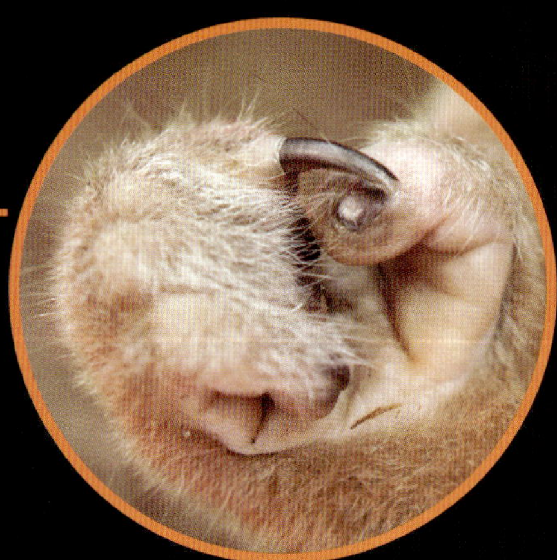

EYES
large, round eyes provide
stereoscopic, or 3D, vision
NOSE
sharp sense of smell
helps locate food

GLOSSARY

ARTHROPODS
animals such as spiders and insects

NOCTURNAL
active at night

TROPICAL
hot and humid

VENOM
a poison produced by an animal's body

FORAGE
to search widely for food

PRIMATES
mammals (animals with hair or fur that feed their babies milk) with gripping hands and a large brain; most primates live in trees

READ MORE

Curtis, Jennifer Keats. *Primate School*. Mt. Pleasant, S.C.: Arbordale, 2015.

Katz Cooper, Sharon. *L is for Lemur: ABCs of Endangered Primates*. North Mankato, Minn.: Capstone Press, 2017.

Shea, Mary Molly. *Poisonous Slow Lorises*. New York: Gareth Stevens, 2018.

WEBSITES

Bristol Zoo Gardens: Slow Loris
https://www.bristolzoo.org.uk/explore-the-zoo/slow-loris

Duke Lemur Center: Slow Loris
https://lemur.duke.edu/slow-loris/

Lincoln Park Zoo: Pygmy Slow Loris
https://www.lpzoo.org/animal/pygmy-slow-loris

Note: Every effort has been made to ensure that the websites listed above are suitable for children, that they have educational value, and that they contain no inappropriate material. However, because of the nature of the Internet, it is impossible to guarantee that these sites will remain active indefinitely or that their contents will not be altered.

INDEX

PUBLISHED BY CREATIVE EDUCATION AND CREATIVE PAPERBACKS

P.O. Box 227, Mankato, Minnesota 56002
Creative Education and Creative Paperbacks are imprints of The Creative Company
www.thecreativecompany.us

LIBRARY OF CONGRESS CATALOGING-IN-PUBLICATION DATA

Names: Arnold, Quinn M., author.
Title: Slow lorises / Quinn M. Arnold.
Series: Creatures of the night.
Includes index.
Summary: Peer into the nocturnal Southeast Asian tropical forests with this high-interest introduction to the venomous primates known as slow lorises.

Identifiers: LCCN: 2018059120
ISBN 978-1-64026-120-4 (hardcover)
ISBN 978-1-62832-683-3 (pbk)
ISBN 978-1-64000-238-8 (eBook)

Subjects: LCSH: Slow loris—Juvenile literature.
Nocturnal animals—Juvenile literature.
Classification: LCC QL737.P955 A76 2019 / DDC 599.8—dc23

CCSS: RI.1.1-6; RI.2.1-7; RF.1.1-4; RF.2.1-4

DESIGN AND PRODUCTION

by Joe Kahnke; art direction by Rita Marshall
Printed in China

PHOTOGRAPHS by Alamy (Paul Bolotov, Ian Butler Photography), Getty Images (John Giustina/Photographer's Choice RF), iStockphoto (bsd555), Minden Pictures (Ch'ien Lee, Andrew Walmsley/NPL), National Geographic Image Collection (JOEL SARTORE/NATIONAL GEOGRAPHIC PHOTO ARK), Shutterstock (Shpak Anton, Maria Arts, Chaitawat.P, hkhtt hj, Stephen Marques, Melin Creative, Seregraff)

Image on page 20 courtesy of Perth Zoo.

FIRST EDITION HC 9 8 7 6 5 4 3 2 1
FIRST EDITION PBK 9 8 7 6 5 4 3 2 1